PLAYSKOOL ®

My Nose, My Toes!

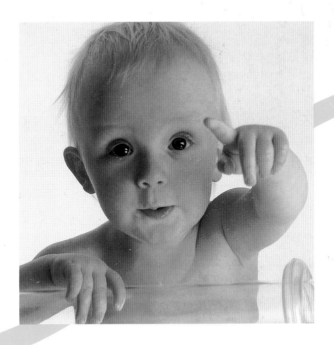

PLAYSKOOL® BOOKS

An Imprint of Dutton Children's Books ● New York

eyes

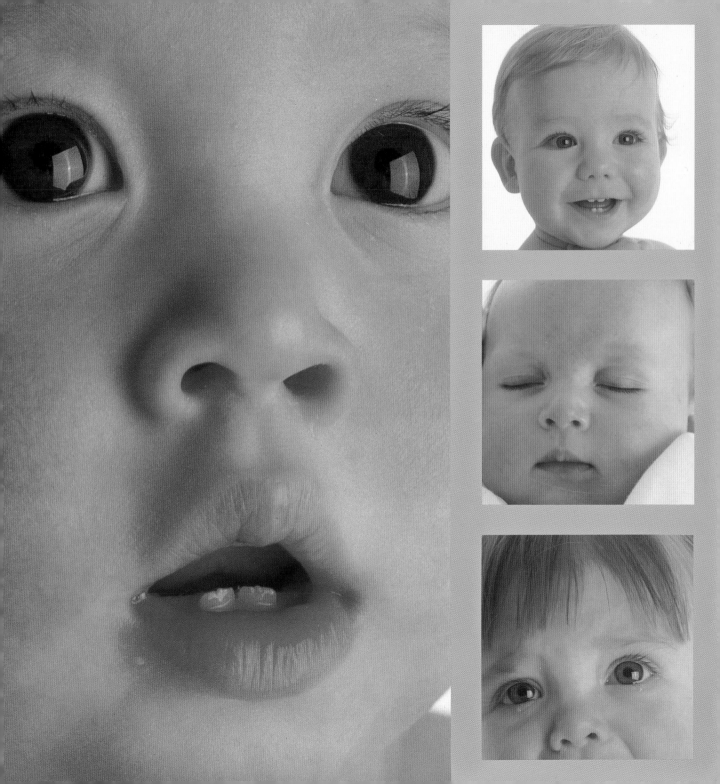

nose

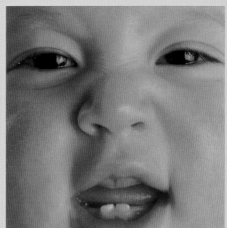

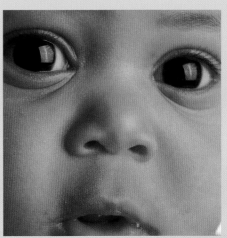

mouth

ears

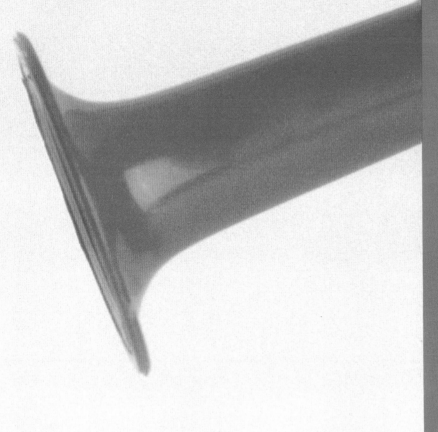

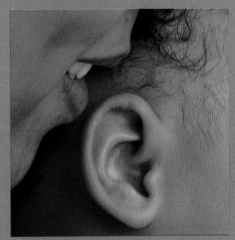

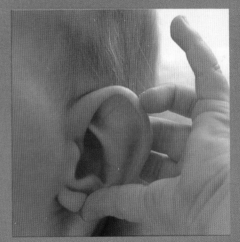

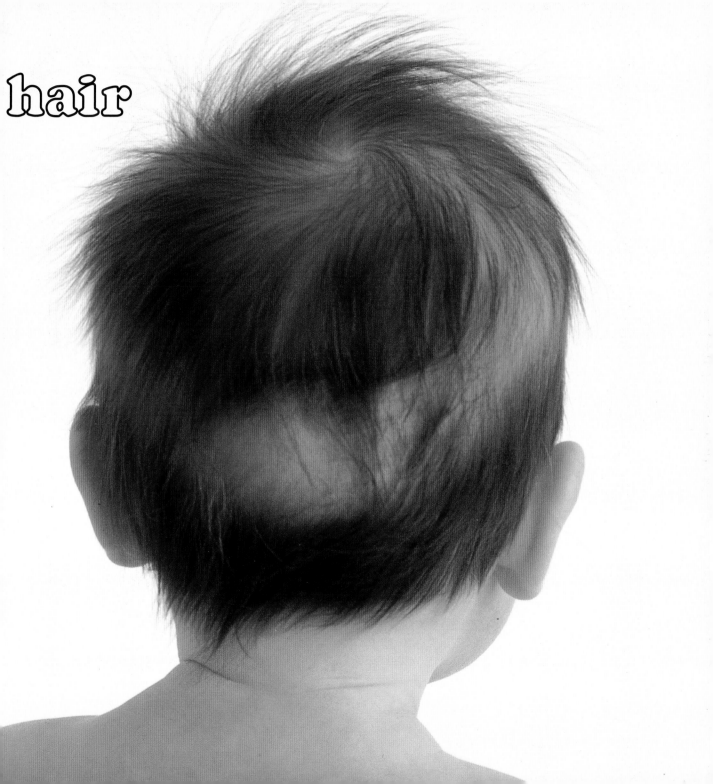

hair

arms

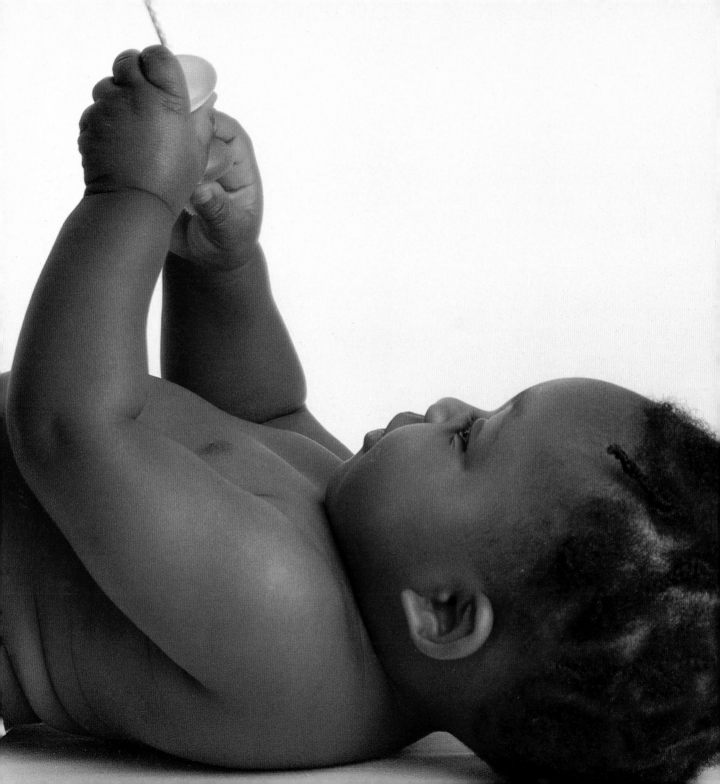

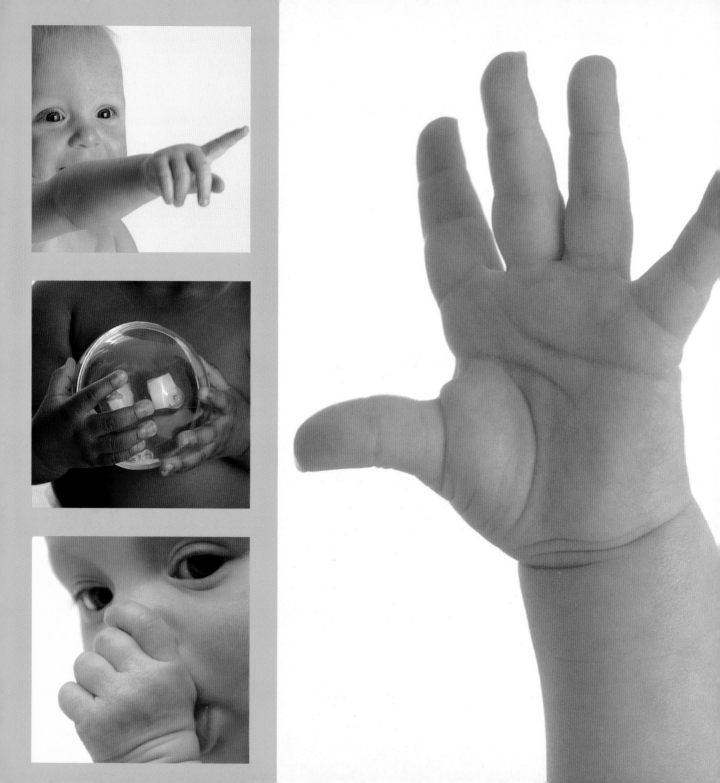

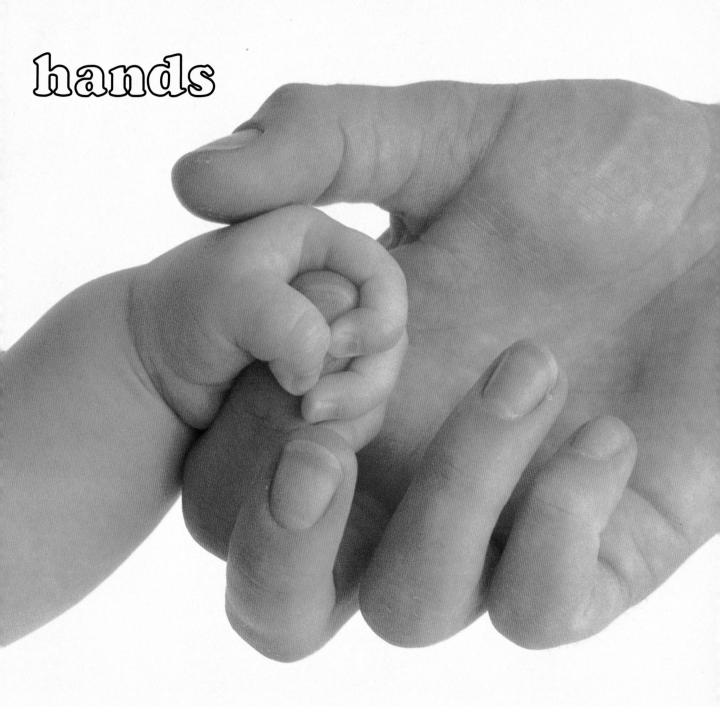

hands

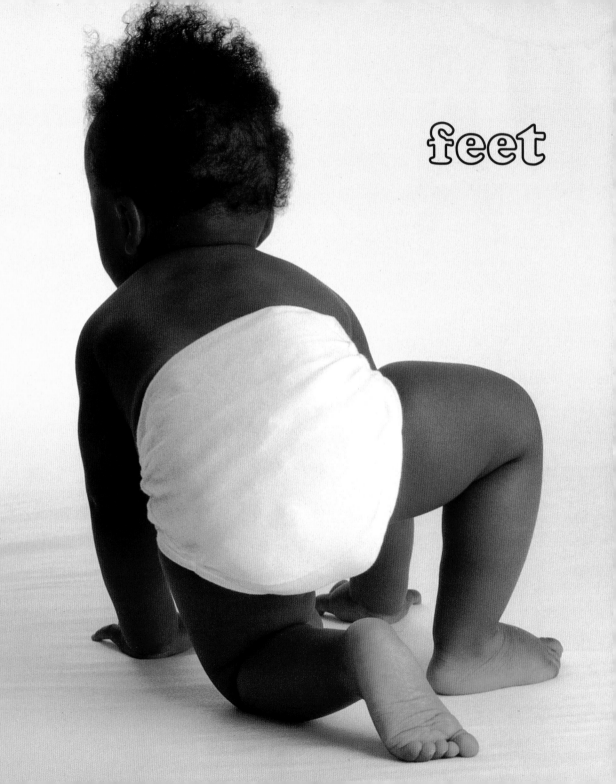

feet

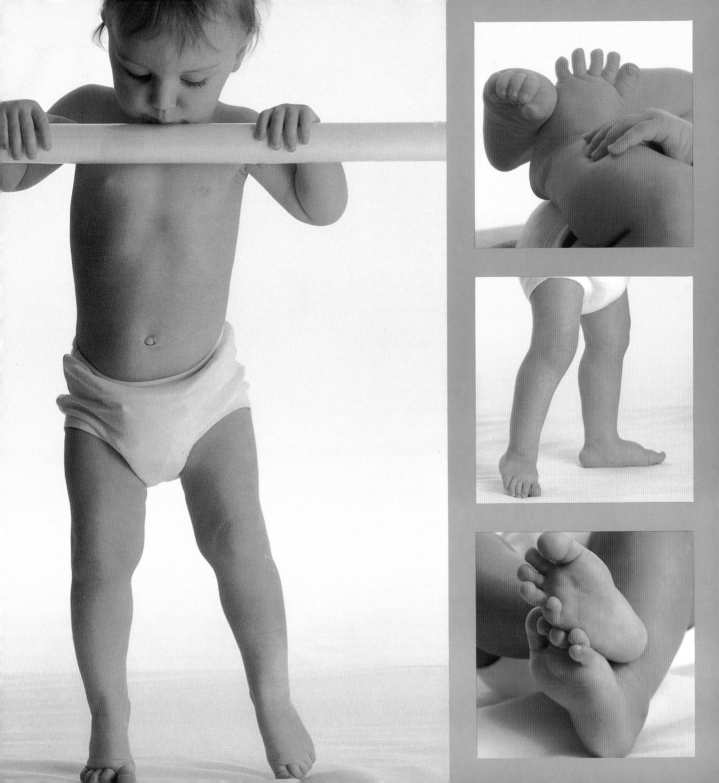

eyes

nose

mouth

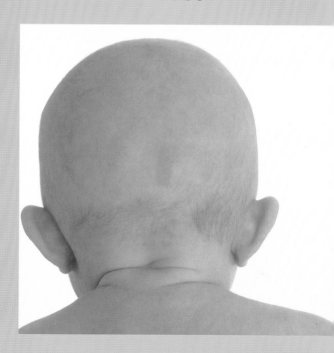

ears

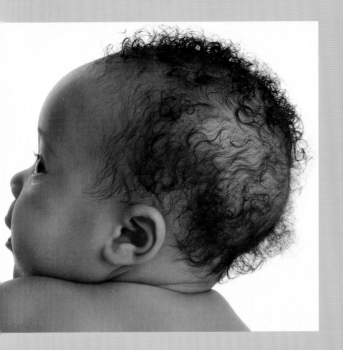

hair

arms

hands

feet

Published in the United States 1995
by Dutton Children's Books,
a division of Penguin Books USA Inc.
375 Hudson Street, New York, New York 10014

Originally published 1994 by William Heinemann Ltd.,
a division of Reed International Books Ltd., London.

First American Edition ISBN O-525-45472-1
Manufactured in United States of America
10 9 8 7 6 5 4